The
Frail
Days

ORCA
limelights

The
Frail
Days

Gabrielle
Prendergast

ORCA BOOK PUBLISHERS

Library and Archives Canada Cataloguing in Publication

Prendergast, Gabrielle, author
The frail days / Gabrielle Prendergast.
(Orca limelights)

Issued in print and electronic formats.
ISBN 978-1-4598-0464-7 (pbk.).—ISBN 978-1-4598-0465-4 (pdf).—
ISBN 978-1-4598-0466-1 (epub)

I. Title. II. Series: Orca limelights
PS8631.R448F73 2015   jc813'.6   c2014-906669-4
c2014-906670-8

First published in the United States, 2015
Library of Congress Control Number: 2014952058

Summary: Stella and her newly formed band must decide whether to change
their edgy rock sound to get into a conservative summer music festival.

*Orca Book Publishers is dedicated to preserving the environment and has
printed this book on Forest Stewardship Council® certified paper.*

Orca Book Publishers gratefully acknowledges the support for
its publishing programs provided by the following agencies:
the Government of Canada through the Canada Book Fund and the
Canada Council for the Arts, and the Province of British Columbia
through the BC Arts Council and the Book Publishing Tax Credit.

Cover design by Rachel Page
Cover photography by Getty Images

ORCA BOOK PUBLISHERS   ORCA BOOK PUBLISHERS
PO Box 5626, STN. B   PO Box 468
Victoria, BC Canada   Custer, WA USA
v8R 6s4   98240-0468

www.orcabook.com
Printed and bound in Canada.

18 17 16 15 • 4 3 2 1

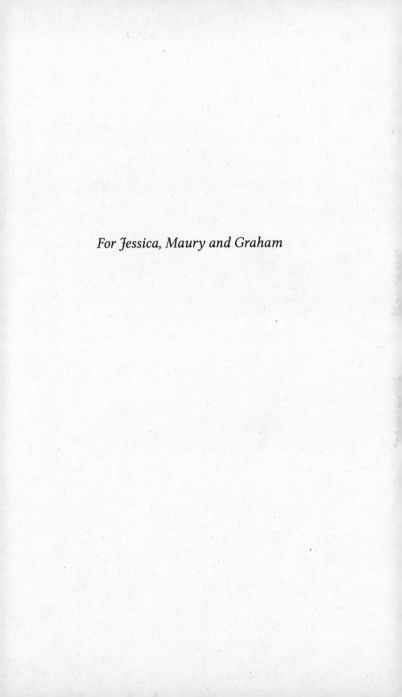

For Jessica, Maury and Graham

One

"**N**ext!"

I don't say it loud enough for the bimbo with the Disney Princess cartoon voice to hear me. She's halfway back out to her boyfriend's truck by now anyway. Probably about to tell him what a great audition she did. How she's sure to get the gig and join our *adorable* band. She actually said that: "You guys are so *adorable!*" I wanted to tell her the great lengths I have gone not to be adorable. Pierced nose. Fire-engine-red hair. Doc Martens. A different fake tattoo on my shoulder every week. Vintage T-shirts and black skinny jeans. Leather jacket. I know I'm pretty small for a sixteen-year-old girl, but adorable? Barf.

Mom calls my look "nihilist chic," "neo-punk" and "post-everything." As far as punk goes, she should know. She was there the first time punk came around, even had a mohawk, probably the first Chinese Canadian punk girl ever. She still has all the old records. The Clash. The Sex Pistols. The Dead Kennedys. It's wicked cool, though obviously I'd never tell her that. Dad, meanwhile, used to build his own synthesizers and listen to New Order. Both my parents are way more conservative now. A teacher and an engineer. And, of course, they have to tell me "music today is nothing but noise" every once in a while. But even they would have thought the cartoon girl was awful.

"She wasn't that bad," Miles says. He's pretty diplomatic for a fourteen-year-old who hasn't even hit puberty yet. Maybe he just liked the look of the cartoon girl. But I'm not entirely convinced that he's going to go for girls when his voice finally changes and he grows some armpit hair.

"Are you kidding?" Jacob says. Jacob is the same age as Miles and only a few hormones further along in the puberty department. "She was so sweet I think I'm going into diabetic shock." His voice squeaks on the word *diabetic*.

I try not to laugh. Miles and Jacob hate it when I tease them about being little boys. And fair enough. Between the two of them they've got enough rocker chops to reduce Justin Bieber to a watery puddle of maple syrup. Jacob on guitar and Miles on bass have turned out to be a miracle match for me, despite their tender age. With me on drums, we pump out a rock sound straight from 1978—real guitars, real amps and real drums. Feedback, power chords, thumping bass and banging snare. It's nothing like the hip-hop and country twang that has cast a clichéd cloud over this sad little nowhere town. Miles and Jacob love old rock and punk, the seventies, the eighties, the Seattle grunge of the nineties, even some recent good stuff, as much as I do. Totally in synch in our tastes, we're a dream team. Except for one thing.

As if to illustrate our deprived situation, Miles starts to sing. He sounds like a soloist in the Vienna Boys' Choir. Pretty, but hardly compatible with guitar rock. Jacob is even worse. Puberty has turned his voice into an unpredictable mess, like a piano with half the keys broken, missing or tuned wrong. He and Miles think it's funny as hell, but to me it just reinforces the fact that

I can't sing either. I mean, I have an okay voice. It's just that, in front of more than two people I start to squeak like a mouse. I can't seem to pull it together. If I could, we wouldn't be having this problem.

"The problem is," Jacob says, like he's reading my mind, "every person who wants to sing in a band is either a poser or a diva or a wanker."

"Oh, you noticed?" I say. This morning we've jammed with no fewer than ten aspiring vocalists for our band. Two were not-very-talented rappers. Three couldn't sing at all, even with their giggling friends egging them on. One was a forty-nine-year-old opera singer. She was awesome, actually, but *really*? She had her baby *grandson* with her. Three others were okay singers—just okay. But their tastes ran so close to the middle of the road, I'm surprised they haven't been run over by a truck. If I have to hear someone sing "Viva la Vida" again, I'm going to cry. Then there was Disney Princess singer. She sounded like she was in a contest for the loudest, most emotive diva in the world, competing against Celine Dion and Mariah Carey. Big voice, big boobs, no soul. Thanks but no thanks.

"Maybe we could be an instrumental act," Miles suggests, giving up on his cherubic solo.

"Name an instrumental act that anyone has heard of or cares about," I say.

"The London Philharmonic," Jacob quips.

I flick a guitar pick at him.

"Miles Davis," Miles says, predictably. He's named after Miles Davis, and he actually looks a bit like him. He can even play most of his jazz tunes.

"Both of you, bite me," I say, clambering out from behind the drum kit. It's hot in this garage/ excuse for a studio that we rehearse in. We've been here for hours and we still don't have a singer. I need coffee and air and, most of all, sugar. The real kind. Not the kind the Princess girl was serving.

* * *

I hate the mall and everything it stands for. But it's air-conditioned. And summer seems to have arrived early this year. So it's the best place to go for my caffeine and sugar fix. I couldn't convince the boys to come with me. I don't mind though.

I'm an only child, so I'm used to doing stuff by myself. I stride past the girly boutiques, slowing down only to look at a cool pair of purple Chucks that I don't really need. I have three pairs of Chucks already. In the food court I combine my addictions into a giant iced-coffee extravaganza. I slurp it back in the bookstore, browsing the music section. It's mostly books about country singers and rappers. Like I care about their plastic lives.

I'm about to take a closer look at a book about concert posters when an announcement comes over the PA system.

"Attention, shoppers. Please join us for a special performance by our own Fantalicious! Two o'clock in the central forecourt."

I suppress the urge to gag. Fantalicious is a ridiculous girl group put together by one of the local dance studios and the radio station. The girls wriggle their butts and lip-synch to their own Auto-Tuned voices in malls and supermarkets all over the district. It's disgusting and tragic. Of course, I have to go and check it out.

By the time I get to the forecourt, the speakers are already pumping out a fake bassy rhythm. Fantalicious is "singing" about a cute boy and his hot car. Ugh. They are so embarrassing to every part of me that's female. The four members pose and wiggle through three more sound-alike songs before, mercifully, stopping. Then they mingle with the crowd and sign autographs for the tweeniboppers who squealed through the whole performance. I don't remember being like that when I was a tween. I asked for Pink Floyd's *Dark Side of the Moon* for my ninth birthday. For my tenth I got *Regatta de Blanc* by the Police. For my eleventh I finally got my own MP3 player. After that I downloaded whatever I wanted. Never anything like Fantalicious though. God no.

As I lurk about, watching the fan frenzy, I wonder what it would be like to be mobbed like that. Part of me wants to be famous, but I don't know if I could handle all the attention. I don't even like answering questions in class. But I love music. I want to do it for real. I hate to admit it, but I was a tiny bit jealous of Fantalicious as they were performing. I wonder if they know how silly they are and just don't care. The little kids love them. Maybe that's all that matters.

As the crowd disperses I see Chad Banner sitting behind a table, handing out CDs and posters. *Chad Freakin' Banner.* Even though he's probably only twentysomething, he's the big music czar in town. As well as promoting various acts, he owns the one decent nightclub and deejays a pretty cool Sunday-night radio show. I recognize him from his bus-stop ads. Hopped up on caffeine and sugar as I am, I don't even hesitate to go over to talk to him. I mean, musicians need to schmooze, right? Plus, Chad is sort of hot, for an older guy.

But when I get there, I can't think of anything even remotely cool to say. "What are the T-shirts?" I finally ask, leaning against the table. No way am I going home with a Fantalicious CD, but the black T-shirts might be all right.

"Just for the station. CZLL," he says with a smile. "Want one?"

I take an extra-extra small. "Didn't Fantalicious used to have five members?" I remember seeing them on the local morning show last Christmas, singing lame-o dance-y Christmas carols in stupid sexy elf outfits.

"One of the members dropped out," Chad says. "They haven't had time to replace her." He looks me up and down. "Do you sing?"

Gross. Even if I did...gross.

"I'm only sixteen years old," I say. My parents would buy a minivan before they'd let me prance around dressed like that. And they are *never* going to buy a minivan.

"The girl who quit was only fifteen."

Ew! Double gross.

"I'm not into fluff pop. And I don't sing. I'm a drummer."

"A girl drummer, huh? Cool. You have a band?"

Chad Banner asked me if I have a band. *The* Chad Banner. What can I do? I lie, of course. "I have an awesome band. We're like early Green Day meets Paramore." Where in hell did I get that from? I don't even like Paramore or Green Day.

Chad seems unconcerned about or unaware of my ridiculous lie. "That sounds sweet," he says. "You should try out for the Parkland Summer Music Festival. I'm one of the selectors this year."

This would be a moment to flirt my way into an awesome gig, I guess. But I suck at flirting. Every time I've tried, the boy has practically run screaming in the other direction. "Maybe we will," I say instead. That seems safe enough. I ball the CZLL T-shirt up in my sweaty hands and turn away.

"Hey, what's your name?" Chad says as I start to leave.

"Stella Wing," I say. Strictly speaking, it's Wang, but it's Chinese, right? And we're speaking English. I can pronounce it any way I want. And Wing is just cooler.

"See you at tryouts, Stella Wing," Chad says, turning to sign an autograph for a guy on crutches.

I try to put the idea of the summer festival out of my mind. I mean, he was just teasing me, wasn't he? Right?

Now I *really* need to find a singer.

Two

"Where are we going?"

I feel like we've been riding our bikes forever. I'm in good shape, but I hate bike riding when I actually need to get somewhere. It's fun to just cruise around, but for some reason a destination ruins it. Still, with no car and no driver's license, it's the best way to get places. Better than the bus anyway.

We're already on the outskirts of town. The sun is beating down. Jacob rides way ahead of Miles and me, with his guitar slung over his back. He looks like a traveling minstrel on a ten-speed.

Miles pulls up beside me. He has an expensive mountain bike that's just a little bit too big for him. Since his fashion taste tends to the scruffy, he sometimes looks like a homeless kid who has just stolen some rich teenager's bike. But he *is* a rich teenager. His parents are both doctors.

"It's Mackenzie Field. Out past the airport," he says.

Airport. Airstrip is more like it. Only about two planes land there per day. And one of them is full of fish and peaches from the coast.

"Why are you taking me to a baseball game?" I ask for the tenth time.

"It's a surprise!" Jacob yells back. How he can hear me from that far away is a mystery. With all the loud music he listens to, you'd think he'd be deaf by now.

We ride past the airport just as a small private plane lands. The boys stop to watch, whooping and hollering as the plane swoops low over their heads. Then they race to catch up with me.

"Juvenile much?" I ask them, grinning.

"You're only young once," Jacob says. "Live a little."

Mackenzie Field is a wide, dry, dusty excuse for a sports venue. It's fenced to keep coyotes out and regularly checked for ankle-breaking gopher holes. Apart from that, you could hardly say it's a shining example of civic pride. The stands and dugouts, such as they are, rise up from the north corner. This means the sun blazes into your face the whole time you're watching a game. In the south corner there are three sad little billboards. Two for fast food. One for a funeral home. That always makes me laugh.

The concession stand sells stale donuts and warm soda. I'm pretty sure the donuts are left over from when I played baseball here when I was little. It was depressing even then. And I was a happy kid, more or less.

"Quick, the game's about to start," Jacob says as we lock our bikes under the bleachers. I follow the boys up into the stands. We find seats behind a family of five, all of whom turn around and stare at my hair and piercings for at least a minute. Just as the family turns back, a voice comes over the crackly PA. "*Ladies and gentlemen, please stand for the national anthem.*"

We stand. A girl who looks vaguely familiar walks out onto the field and stands in front of the microphone. She's sort of chubby and has shoulder-length blond hair. In khaki capris and a pale green polo shirt, she doesn't look any older than me, but she's dressed like my grandma. This can't be good, I think.

I wait for the canned musical accompaniment to start, but it doesn't. The girl takes a deep breath and starts to sing.

Now as national anthems go, ours is pretty hard. I know we all sing it at school and everything, but half the time you're just mouthing the words. Or you have to change octaves in the middle just to get all the notes out. And the thing with national anthems is, you can't go halfhearted. You basically have to give it your all or not bother. That's just the way it is.

A few people around us sing along for a few lines, but then they fall silent. Soon there isn't any noise in the field or stands except for the girl singing. For real, even the grasshoppers stop chirping.

No musical background track. No effects on her voice. A weak-ass PA system and terrible acoustics. And it's just a Little League baseball game. But this girl sings the anthem like she's seeing child soldiers off to war. I swear some people are crying.

I feel like crying.

Her voice is *supernatural.* Deep and rich and earthy on the low notes. Pure and strong on the high ones. You can tell she's had training, but not too much. Somehow there's a little edge to her style. She makes the anthem jazzy and soulful and poignant and totally, completely *awesome.* When she finishes, the crowd goes wild.

It's a good minute before I can even speak.

"Who is she?" I say as the applause follows her back behind the concession stand. "She doesn't go to our school."

"She goes to Sacred Heart," Miles says. "One of the guys in swim club knows her. He said she'd be here. Tamara Donnelly is her name."

OMG. Now I know why she looked familiar. I recognize the name.

Tamara Donnelly is the missing member of Fantalicious.

*   *   *

That night I drum along to some old Ramones records until Mom comes in and promises she'll make me brownies if I stop and come hang out with her in the kitchen. She's generally supportive of my music. More so if it takes place outside the house. The garage where the boys and I rehearse is behind my dad's office downtown. That's where I keep my good drum kit. We're not allowed to use the garage unless someone is in the office, just in case there's a problem. There's usually someone there every day, even weekends and some evenings, so it works out pretty well. Except tonight they're all at some training thing. So I'm stuck with my backup kit in my room. And after two hours, my mom has had enough.

"Hey, Mom, have you heard of Fantalicious?" I ask as I watch her measure flour and cocoa into a bowl. My mouth is watering already. Brownies are a major weakness of mine.

"Fantalicious? That's the sleazy girl group, right?"

"They did a show at the mall today."

Mom makes a face as she stirs. "Yuck. That must have been awful for you." She hands me the spoon to lick.

"It's hard to tell with all the effects they put on their voices," I say, "but they can't actually *sing*, can they? I mean, without all the Auto-Tune and effects?"

Mom pours the batter into the brownie tin and slides it into the oven. The kitchen starts to fill with warm, cocoa-scented air. "They had one good singer, but I heard she left."

"Tamara Donnelly? How do you know she's a good singer?"

"She sang at a wedding Dad and I went to. Sang 'Because You Loved Me' better than Celine."

"That wouldn't be hard," I say.

Mom laughs. She hates cheesy music as much as I do. Though she doesn't play her punk vinyl much anymore, she rocks out to classics like Queen and the Who in the car—or AC/DC, if she's feeling rebellious. Once she picked me up at school with "You Shook Me All Night Long" cranking out her Volvo windows. It was totally epic.

When the brownies are done, I take three of them and a big glass of milk back to my room. Brownies and milk. I'm so hard-core. Live fast. Eat chocolate. That's my philosophy. I slip on some headphones and line up some Nirvana on my laptop. Then my brownies and I do some heavy googling. I need to know more about Tamara Donnelly.

I find her Facebook page easily enough. We even have a couple of friends in common. But unless I friend her, most of her profile is hidden. She's one of those cautious teens, I guess. That's cool. I am too. I don't want everyone all up in my business all the time.

Next, I find an article about Fantalicious's appearance on the morning show. It's a dumb article that says nothing. Like most Internet "news," I guess. There are a lot of comments, though, most of them pretty supportive. "What nice kids," "So refreshing to see such commitment so young" and whatnot. But some of the comments are critical of their cheeky outfits: short elf dresses with polka-dot tights. A couple of church types call them "lascivious." I have to look that up. Slutty, it means. I pretty much agree. No one comments on the fact that the music was crap. That about sums it up. The music doesn't matter with an act like that.

Next, I find a YouTube video of Tamara singing with a church choir. Jeez, split personality much? Skanky elf versus choir girl? I'm not one for hymns, but by the end of the video,

I'm impressed. Tamara killed her solo. She really can sing. No question.

But Fantalicious? And church music? How would she feel about rocking out with a crazy Chinese drummer and two junior-sized rock gods? Could I show her the error of her ways?

Google doesn't give me the answer to that. But it *does* give me Tamara's choir-rehearsal schedule.

Three

The number 12 bus smells funny. It just does. Mom says it smelled funny before I was even born, when she rode it out to the school for work. Now it smells like a combination of Chinese food and bleach. Sometimes it's more like banana peels and chalk dust. I know it's not always the same bus. I've seen the bus depot, and there are at least a dozen buses that shuttle people around this magnificent smallopolis we call our hometown. Surely each bus rotates through the number 12 route. It can't always be the same one. But it always smells.

I've ridden the other bus routes. Neither the number 5 nor the number 8 smell. Only the number 12 smells. It's freaky.

Maybe it's something about the route it takes. It actually does go through what qualifies as Chinatown (two Chinese takeouts and an acupuncturist) and past the industrial laundry that does all the hospital washing. So that explains the Chinese food and bleach. The bananas and chalk are a mystery though. I guess some mysteries are just meant to go unsolved.

"What are you spacing out about?" Miles says, nudging me. We're riding the number 12 to the other side of town. On a kind of quest. Like the Fellowship of the Ring. Only with fewer fellows.

"Bananas," I answer.

"Cryptic," Jacob says. As usual, he's strumming his acoustic guitar. The bus is half empty and we're sitting right at the back, spread out on the long bench. Miles has a guitar with him too. A tiny little half-size classical. I don't know why the boys brought their guitars along on this trip. We're going to listen to music, not play it. I guess they just can't live without them.

At the next stop, about ten teenage girls get on board, slouching into the seats just in front of us. Jacob begins playing a guitar riff. Loud.

Really twanging it. I recognize it, of course. It's U2, "Sunday Bloody Sunday."He plays it a couple of times, then stops, looking at me expectantly.

Okay. The song actually starts with drums. One of the few songs that does. I pull some drumsticks out of my backpack. Yeah, so, I never leave home without them. So what? I start playing the distinctive drum pattern using the metal handle on the back of the seat and the soft seat cushion as high-hat cymbal and snare. Jacob smiles and begins the guitar riff again as some of the girls turn and look back at us. Miles starts plucking out fat bass chords. Soon we have a good little jam going.

U2 is pretty corny, but this is a good song to do acoustically on the back of a bus, I'll give them that. And lots of kids know it, even dorky kids. Sure enough, soon a couple of the girls are singing along, half in tune and half laughing. By the time we get to the chorus, the whole back of the bus is shouting, "SUNDAY BLOODY SUNDAAAAAAY!" and "HOW LONG? HOW LONG MUST WE SING THIS SONG?"

Jacob, Miles and I are trying not to laugh. These girls are all done up to go and hang out at the mall or something, and here they are, belting out this 1980s protest song about Northern Ireland. But they seem to be enjoying it. And some of them even know all the words. By the time we get to the mall and the song ends, they're all squealing and telling us how great we are. Jacob is flirting like crazy, though all the girls are at least two years older than him.

When the girls finally pile out, the bus driver turns and looks back at us. "Do you know 'I Will Follow'?" he says.

I guess there are some cool people in this town. All you have to do to find them is ride the number 12 bus.

If you can stand the smell.

*   *   *

We get out at the second-to-last stop and walk two blocks down a row of large houses to a modern-looking church at the end. The sign outside the church reads *Free Coffee and Everlasting Life.*

"It should say 'free coffee OR everlasting life,'" Miles says as we head for the front door. "Then we'd find out who the real believers are."

Jacob snorts with laughter. I shush them both as I push the heavy wooden door open.

Inside, the church is infused with a weird rainbow light, because the setting sun is beaming in through the stained-glass windows. The pews are empty. There's no service on right now, just choir practice. I see Tamara look over at us as we slip into a pew, as quietly as possible. The choir is in the middle of singing something about eagles' wings. Tamara isn't singing a solo or anything, but I can still pick her voice out from those of the other girls and women. It's strong and clear, but also, in this song anyway, other-worldly. Like she's singing from a mythical land.

But it's church music. The type of music I want to do is about more than just hitting the notes. It's about believing in it. I wonder whether Tamara could believe in anything but the stuff she's used to.

As the eagle song finishes, I hear the door open behind us. A cute but geeky guy comes in and waves to Tamara. She waves back. Boyfriend? Figures. They match each other.

The choir director says something I can't hear, but it makes the whole choir chatter with enthusiasm. After riffling through their music for a moment, they start a new song.

I don't recognize it at first. It sounds African. Then half the choir starts making this kind of heartbeat *whoomph* sound, like a rhythm. And Tamara starts to sing solo.

As soon as the first words are out of her mouth, I recognize the song. It's "Biko," by Peter Gabriel. I've got no idea why they are singing a song about apartheid in South Africa in a church on the other side of the world. But it's straight-up *off the hook*. Her voice is so spectacular, and the acoustics are so good, I feel like I might have found God.

When the choir comes in on the chorus, "Oh Biko, Biko, because Biko," for real I almost pee my pants. And you can tell, I can tell, Miles can tell, Jacob can tell, the cute guy behind us can tell—heck, the statue of Jesus can tell—that Tamara believes in every word and every note she's singing.

There is no question in my mind that she's my singer. I must have this girl in my band. Now I just have to convince her.

When the song ends and my heart rate slowly returns to normal, Tamara comes back to talk to us.

"Looking to join the choir?" she asks. "We always need new singers."

"We can't sing," we all say at once.

Tamara grins. "Are you guys triplets or something?"

Good, I think. A sense of humor helps.

"Hey, Tam," the cute boy behind us says. "We should go. I'm illegally parked."

"Okay. Wait for me?"

He leaves, chatting with the choir director and holding the door for some of the older singers. Tamara, the boys and I exchange names.

"So," Tamara says. "You're not here to join choir. What are you here for?"

"We have a band," I say before I lose my nerve. "We need a singer."

I'm not sure what kind of reaction I expected. Laughter maybe. Or eagerness. Or something. Instead, Tamara just frowns.

"We heard you sing at the baseball game," Jacob says. "You're really good."

"Yeah, thanks." She crosses her arms over her shapeless gray cardigan. "Look, I have to go. Why don't you email me or something?" She fishes a

pen and a slip of paper from her purse and scrib-
bles her details, handing the paper to me.

"I love to sing. I guess you figured that out,
but..." She looks at the boy still holding the door
open. He gestures for her to hurry. "I'm in a
weird place right now. But, you know, email me.
I'll think about it."

The choir director hustles us all out the door
and locks it behind us. Tamara and the boy get
into a perfectly boring car and drive off. Miles,
Jacob and I stand on the church steps like
orphans.

"A weird place?" I say. "What does that mean?"

Four

Dear Tamara

PLEEEEEEEEEASE be our singer. Please please please please please please please please infinity please googolplex pleeeeeeezzzzeeee.

Stella

Too much maybe? I delete the email and try again.

Dear Tamara,

With regards to the proposal we discussed this Saturday last, please be advised that...

What the funk? Who am I, Jane Austen?

Yo, Tam girl

Wassup? When u gonna jam wit me and my boyz?

I laugh so hard, Mom knocks on my door to see if I'm dying.

"Fine! I'm fine!" When I catch my breath, I try one last time.

Hi Tamara

I'm going to Vinyl Village tomorrow morning, elevenish. Wanna come? We can talk.

Best

Stella

An hour later, after I've checked my emails so many times I'm getting repetitive strain injury in my mouse finger, I get this reply.

Stella

VV sounds fun. CU at 11.

T

I hate people who write "see you" as "CU" but at this point, I can't let it be a deal breaker.

It's easy enough to find Tamara in Vinyl Village the next day, because she's the only person in there wearing beige. I mean, *beige.* Seriously? But Mom always says not to judge an album by the liner notes, or something, so whatever. Since Tamara can sing like the love child of Annie Lennox and David Bowie, she can wear all the beige she wants. Heck, *I'll* wear beige if she wants me to.

"Hi, Stella," she says when I join her by the country albums. "I haven't been here in ages. Do you buy a lot of vinyl?"

"Yeah," I say. "My parents have a pretty big vinyl collection. But they like to add to it. So I've been coming here with them since I was a baby."

"Hey, Stella! 'Sup?" the guy behind the counter says, on cue. For a second I worry that Tamara might think I'm showing off, but then two twelve-year-old girls pull out phones and start taking pictures of her and giggling, whispering, "Fantalicious" to each other. Tamara turns away and heads down the jazz aisle.

"I bet that gets irritating," I say, thinking how awesome it might be to be recognized like that. To have giggling fans taking pictures. That would mean they like your music, right?

"Yeah, it was okay when I was still with the group," Tamara says. "But now it's just humiliating. I mean, they're probably making fun of me."

I don't know what to say for a moment. Apart from the fact that I don't really know what she's talking about, Tamara seems sad suddenly. I feel like I should say something supportive, which will probably cause a short circuit in my brain because I'm useless at stuff like that.

But then Tamara pulls out a record and gasps. "Oh my god. I've been looking for this for ages!"

I look at the album. It's a live recording of Billie Holiday. Tamara literally hugs it to her chest.

"Billie Holiday?" I say. "You like her?" I don't listen to much jazz, but Mom and Dad put it on some nights when they're mellowing out on the deck with wine and their weird friends. Billie Holiday is one of my favorites because she's just so depressing. It's awesome music for angsty chocolate binges.

"I *love* her!" Tamara says. "Of course I love her. Any female singer who doesn't worship and admire her is a faker as far as I'm concerned. Doesn't matter what style you're singing, Billie can teach you something. You don't even need to be a singer. Anyone with a soul can learn from Billie Holiday."

I can't help grinning. That's the type of thing I would say about drummers and Stewart Copeland or Travis Barker. "Who else do you like?" I ask.

We spend nearly an hour talking about Aretha Franklin and Janis Joplin. Tamara schools me about Patsy Cline and Mahalia Jackson. And I hook her up with Chrissie Hynde and P.J. Harvey. We have a brief argument about Adele versus Amy Winehouse, which is only resolved when she points out that Adele is in fact still alive and thus wins by default. After giggling for about ten minutes about how dumb that logic is, we nearly have to flip a coin about a really-good-condition German EP of "Push It" by Salt-N-Pepa. I let her have it—I can't be seen with hip-hop, even though it is a cool song.

"So why'd you quit Fantalicious anyway?" I ask as she pays for her albums. Her happy mood seems to evaporate. She tucks her wallet away and swishes the shopping bag off the counter. I practically have to run to catch up with her.

Outside the store, Tamara stops and stares up at the sky. She looks miserable.

"Hey, what's up?" I say.

"I didn't quit," Tamara says. "They pretty much kicked me out."

"What?! They must be insane!"

"Thanks," Tamara says. We start walking toward the bus stop. "They kept having meetings without me. Then one day our manager turned up with these new costumes and..."

I wait. It feels like the right thing to do. Maybe I'm not so hopeless at interpersonal relations after all. We walk half a block before Tamara speaks again.

"None of them fit me," she says, blushing. "And Petra, that's our manager, said they didn't come in bigger sizes. So..."

I feel sick. And a little guilty. When we saw Tamara singing at the baseball game, I thought to myself that she was chubby. And she *is* a bit chubby, but not in a bad way. And anyway, that's no reason for her not to be in a singing group. It's no reason to be excluded from anything. "That's discrimination," I say. "They can't fire you for not fitting into some cheesy cheerleader bunny suit."

Tamara laughs then. "Thanks," she says. "So whatever. I guess I did quit rather than face that humiliation again. It sucks, because I wanted to sing at the festival this summer and they're probably going to headline. But Petra kept telling me about diets and exercises I could do, and I tried some, but...I'm just not a skinny little tart."

"Like me?" I say.

"You're not a tart, Stella. You have class."

Class? That's a first. But I like it. "Our band will be the classiest group in town," I say. "Sing for us, Tamara, please. We're not sizeist, ageist, racist, sexist or homophobic. We'll even let you choose your own clothes. And *we're* going to try out for the festival. Maybe they'll choose us to headline." She still looks uncertain. So I try my pleading face. It works on Dad when I need extra iTunes money. Sometimes it even works on Mom. I don't think Tamara is so easily moved. So I try something softer. "Just come and jam with us, Tamara. What have you got to lose?"

"Nothing, I guess," she says. "Nothing but pride—and after a year with Fantalicious, I'm used to throwing that away."

* * *

"What about 'Viva la Vida'?" Miles says. He even plunks out the opening chords on our keyboard.

"Seriously, Miles? I'll kill you," I say.

Tamara snorts into her Slurpee. "It's not a great singer's song anyway. How about something old? I think I could probably fake my way through 'Stairway to Heaven.'"

"As much as I would love that," Jacob says, "I'm not sure anyone should ever fake that song."

I exchange a look with the boys. Tamara seems different now we're talking about her singing. Confident. Almost arrogant. It's a little irritating. I mean, I know she's a good singer and all, but she doesn't have to be so cocky. Faking "Stairway to Heaven"! Really?

"Shouldn't we be thinking of a girl singer?" I say. This whole process is beginning to frustrate me. Tamara has been in the studio for twenty minutes and we haven't played a note.

"I can sing tenor range too, but whatever." Tamara drops her empty Slurpee cup into the overflowing trash and picks up the iPod from the

35

top of Jacob's amp. "What about Tracy Bonham? She's a girl."

"You know 'Mother Mother'?" I ask.

Miles coughs explosively, and Jacob frowns at me, but Tamara doesn't even twitch.

"Give me five minutes and some headphones and I'll be good," she says, taking the iPod and headphones outside to sit in the sun.

As soon as the door closes, Jacob sighs. "Why'd you choose such a hard song?"

"It's not hard. We play it all the time."

"It's hard to *sing*, Stella," Miles says. "Maybe you could ease her into it a bit?"

"This is a rock band, isn't it? Aren't we trying to find out if she can rock out?"

"Well, yeah, but I don't think we should scare her off. I mean, she's literally our last hope."

He's infuriatingly right. They both are. Now I'm worried that the song will freak her out. Not only is it hard to sing, but it's pretty dark. I start searching through my phone for something a little lighter while the boys tune up. But before I find anything suitable, Tamara comes back in.

"Ready to roll?" she says. She doesn't look scared. Maybe a little nervous. But I'm terrible at reading emotions.

Jacob starts playing the opening of the song, and Tamara comes in right away, just like she's supposed to. She changes as she sings, loosens up. Her eyes close and she sways a bit, until the song changes and Miles and I come in with bass and drums. Tamara jumps in time with us, clutching the mike, waving her free hand and looking very rock and roll for a girl in pink yoga pants and a Gap cardigan. When she wails out the ironic chorus line "Everything's fine!" with a genuine growly break in her voice, Jacob's eyes almost bug out of his head. Miles just grins.

She doesn't miss a word or a note. She makes me believe every emotion. And she looks *cool.* Somehow the music transforms her into a rough-and-ready rock chick singing about how hard it all is. It's some kind of musical magic. When the song ends we all just sit there silent for a few seconds.

"Well," Jacob finally says. "I vote yes."

"Me too," Miles says. "That was wicked."

I'm smiling like a drunk monkey when I add my vote. "One hundred percent. What do you think, Tamara? Are you in?"

She has a thoughtful look on her face, and for a second I'm worried she's going to tell us she doesn't think we're her scene. But then she grins. "That was the most fun I've had in weeks," she says. "Let's do it again."

Five

Music has a look. Rock, punk, metal, emo, whatever. It's not that you need to be super beautiful (though, hello, it helps), but every type of music has its own look. Maybe it's superficial, but music is a product. And products need to be branded, right? McDonald's couldn't just change the golden arches to pink arches and expect people not to freak out. I'm sure my mom would have plenty to say about the commercialization of cultural experience and the resulting degradation of blah, blah, blah, but they call it the music *business* for a reason.

So if you're playing one type of music, your look should fit with it. It just makes sense. And as much as I think Tamara has a voice and a musical attitude that will set this town on fire, her look reminds me of a soccer mom. In fact, when I played soccer and my mom came to my games, she looked way more rock and roll than Tamara does.

Tamara says she still has all her Fantalicious outfits and that some of them still fit her and more or less cover her lady parts. I'm tempted to throw the whole lot into a vat of black dye and see how that turns out. But the outfits are pretty skimpy. And I hate that skimpily dressed rocker-chick look. Why do female musicians have to prance around half naked just because they're girls? It's not a beauty contest.

I guess it's not a fashion show either. It feels a bit like one, though, because I've been waiting for Tamara to come out of the fitting room for ten minutes. We've already searched through her entire wardrobe, and apart from her Fantalicious clothes and her school uniform (which had a temptingly AC/DC effect), there wasn't much that said Rock Goddess.

"Do you have the skinny jeans on?" I say through the fitting-room door.

"Yeah, but..."

"But what?"

"But butt. My butt looks huge."

"Put the Clash T-shirt on with them."

"Why? Does the Clash have magical butt-shrinking properties?"

The saleslady frowns at me as she folds artfully frayed chinos. I think she's upset that someone is saying "butt" in her store.

"Just come out, Tamara," I say. "Let me see."

Tamara opens the fitting-room door and stands there in the skinny jeans and black T-shirt I picked out. She looks at herself in the giant mirror. "I look sad."

She's right. She does look sad. I may have met the only girl in the world who doesn't look good in black. And the skinny jeans do nothing for her either. An outfit that is practically my uniform, and the only thing I really feel like me in, looks terrible and wrong on her. That's an eye-opener.

"What do you like to wear?" I say through the door as Tamara changes back into her own clothes. "What's your favorite?"

"Pajamas," she says. "And the long robes we wear in the church choir. Hey! Maybe I could wear a burka! That would be a unique look. Or I could dress like a nun." I'm still trying to picture this when she comes out in her own clothes, leaving the jeans and T-shirt behind. "Those are dumb ideas. I would never wear a burka. It's not right to mock other cultures like that. And even nuns don't dress like nuns anymore. I could wear a sari. I mean, not in a mean way either. I think they're lovely. But I wouldn't want to offend anyone. You know, because...I'm going to just shut up now."

I can't help laughing. Soon we're both laughing so hard that the saleslady gives us dirty looks until we leave the store.

"Argh!" Tamara groans as we head up the escalator to the food court. "I hate shopping for clothes. It's so demoralizing. Nothing fits or suits me. I should get a body artist to paint me and perform completely nude."

We howl with laughter all the way to the coffee kiosk. But when we get there, there's a massive lineup.

"The coffee here is awful anyway. Let's go somewhere else."

Tamara leads me out of the mall and down the pedestrian arcade to a little vintage diner at the end. Dad used to take me for breakfast here sometimes when he still worked at city hall. But I haven't been here for ages. It seems to have had a hipster makeover. Jazz is drifting out of a jukebox, and there are posters of detective movies on the walls.

I join Tamara as she takes a seat at the counter. A second later, the cute guy from her choir practice plops two cups in front of us.

"You look desperately in need of caffeine," he says, pouring coffee from a glass pot.

"Stella, this is my brother, Nate," Tamara says.

Her brother? Why does he look cuter all of a sudden? He has little glasses and sandy-brown hair with a cowlick you could park a bike in. His eyes are so blue and bright, he looks like a cartoon version of himself. I reach out to shake his hand and knock over the coffee he's just poured. Seriously? I should just run away right now.

"Don't worry about it." He wipes up the coffee as I apologize. "Tammy tells me you're a drummer. That's pretty cool."

"Yeah," I say. "I mean, thanks. Do you play an instrument?"

"Clarinet. Just in school band though."

Oh dear. That's disappointing. Saxophone would have been better. Still, he makes a good cup of coffee, now that I'm actually drinking one rather than flooding the countertop with it.

When we finish our coffees, Tamara and I hop on the bus and head to the studio. The boys are waiting there for us, Miles playing my drums and Jacob playing Miles's bass.

"Hey, ladies," Jacob says, popping the bass strings. "We thought of a name for the band."

"Here we go," I say. Jacob and Miles come up with about ten names per day, each one more disgusting than the last. "Let's hear it."

"Crustcore," Miles says, embellishing it with a little cymbal flourish.

"Ew," Tamara says. "What does that even mean?"

"It's a terrible name. Next?"

"What about Scum? We could even make it an acronym. Like, Serious Criminals something something. SCUM."

"Stupid Children Using Marijuana?" I suggest.

"Stoned Chimps Under-Motivated?" Tamara offers, not missing a beat.

Jacob and Miles look hurt. "We don't use drugs. This is a drug-free band."

"Scum is a doubleplusdisgusting name."

"Newspeak? George Orwell. Nice," Tamara says, nodding.

"Can you two speak English, please?" Jacob says. "We still need a name."

"What about the Toenails?" I suggest.

"God," Tamara says. "And you thought Scum was disgusting. Why would you want such a negative name? Why not just call us the Screaming Rejects?"

Before the boys can start discussing the merits of that name, someone knocks on the door. Nate pops his head in.

"I finished my shift early. I thought I could take some band pictures."

"Nate, I'm dressed like a kinder-gym teacher," Tamara says.

"No one cares about that," Nate says and proceeds to take about twenty pictures of me before I even have time to fluff up my faux-hawk. "Do some drumming. I'll get some action shots."

I do a big rolling solo as Nate snaps a bunch more pictures.

"That was awesome. I slowed down the speed so the sticks are blurred. Look how cool it is."

He shows me the camera screen, and he's right. It's pretty cool. After I've admired myself for a few minutes, I notice no one else is saying anything. Tamara is standing with her arms crossed. The boys just look awkward.

"I don't mean to be a diva," Tamara says, "but aren't I the lead singer of this band?"

"Don't be so touchy, Tammy," Nate says. "Like you didn't get enough pictures taken with the Fantasy Lickers."

Tamara's face falls. "You. Are. A. Total. Dick," she says. Then she grabs her bag and flounces out the door.

The girl can sure flounce.

"Tammy! Wait," Nate says, following her.

So much for rehearsal. This is why I'm glad I'm an only child.

"Well," Miles says, after we've taken a moment to process what just happened. "I think it's possible Tamara might actually *be* a bit of a diva."

"No she's not," Jacob says. "Nate was making a fool of himself, slobbering all over Stella."

"He wasn't slobbering over me!" Jeez. Was he? That's embarrassing. And oddly intriguing. "He was taking band pictures."

"Yeah? And how many did he take of anyone other than you?"

I know the answer to that. It looks like we might have our first groupie.

Six

I set a different text tone for everyone I know. But I guess I forgot that I set Tamara's tone to be a cat meow. So when I wake up, I think there's an invisible cat in my room, and I'm very confused for about five minutes. That's just what it's like being me. Once I figure out the invisible cat is no threat, I read Tamara's text.

Sorry. Call me.

I press the button, and she picks up after one ring.

"I wanted to apologize for yesterday," she says straight away. "My brother brings out the worst in me sometimes."

"S'okay," I say, scanning my floor for a clean T-shirt. I've had some time to think about it, and I can see why Tamara is feeling sensitive. It must have sucked, getting pushed out of Fantalicious, especially for such a dumb reason. And I don't know what was going on with Nate taking so many pictures of me. I decide not to mention that part. "Calling them the Fantasy Lickers was mean," I say.

"Yeah, I guess. I know it was cheesy, but it was fun. And I miss them." She sighs into the phone. "I just feel like crap right now."

I'm not normally the type of person to follow up someone saying "I feel like crap" with a request for more details. So no one is more surprised than me when I say, "You do? Why?"

"I just...hate my body. I feel ugly and stupid. I really want to be a performer, but I don't have the image. You know? And you're so...like, perfect and cool and..."

"Chinese?"

"That doesn't matter."

"Name a Chinese girl rock drummer."

That stumps her, but only for a second. She counters with "Name a fat pop singer."

"Ann Wilson, Aretha Franklin," I say. "Meatloaf."

"Meatloaf! You're supposed to make me feel better, not worse!"

She's laughing though. That's good.

"Image isn't everything," I say. "The music is what matters. This band is old school, remember? We're going back to the days before video clips and style blogs."

She's quiet for a second. "I'm surprised to hear you say that."

"Why?"

"Well, to be honest, when I met you I thought you might be a bit of a poser. I mean, you've got the hair and the piercings. Lots of kids look a certain way, like rockers or whatever, but they don't know anything about that scene."

"But you don't still think I'm a poser?"

"No way! You're an awesome drummer. And it's wild to sing with a real drummer. Fants only ever used canned music. It's just not the same."

"Right? This is my whole motivation for the band! Real music for real people."

"Totally."

We have one of those silences where you're talking to someone and you know that you both feel exactly the same way about something. You just have to take a moment and enjoy how good that feels. I realize I've been standing in the middle of my room with a pair of red-and-black leggings in one hand and my phone in the other. Also I'm wearing only an oversized Led Zeppelin T-shirt.

"Stella?" Tamara says suddenly. "Can I send you some lyrics? I mean, lyrics I wrote?"

"You write lyrics? I'd love to read them."

"Cool. I'm going to email them. Don't, like, barf or anything. You'll probably think they're dumb."

"Just send them. I promise I'll be nice."

After we hang up, I get dressed, which basic-ally means putting the red-and-black leggings on under the Led Zep tee. Then I open my laptop. Tamara's email has already arrived. She doesn't waste time with salutations or anything. It's just the lyrics.

They're *amazing*. And heartbreaking. Tamara has this air of confidence sometimes, especially about music. But other times she seems so unsure of herself. I guess that's normal—I feel that way most of the time too—but her lyrics just capture it. The song is called "The Alien," and it's kind of a story about someone who can't hide the fact that they're from another planet. And the more they try, the more people shun them. The last verse of the song is about the alien falling in love with someone who can't love them back.

Wow. I have tears in my eyes when I finish reading. I pick up my phone and text one word back to Tamara.

GENIUS.

She replies in seconds with a happy face.

Normally I hate happy faces, but it's nice to see her smile.

* * *

The boys hunch over the printout I made of Tamara's lyrics while Tamara and I open all the studio windows. The neighbors usually don't complain about the noise so early in the day, and it's hotter than Tabasco in the studio, so we decide to risk it.

"Something like Nine Inch Nails?" Miles says. "Sort of slow and rolling?" He plucks out a few bass notes in an interesting progression.

"Nah, it needs to be darker," Jacob says. "Like 'Creep' only not so emo. And more minor chords."

He strums a chord, then taps a pedal with his foot. His guitar is nice and distorted when he plays the second chord. Miles nods in agreement as Jacob plucks out some killer intro riffs.

"Nice," he says as they continue jamming.

"I'm not sure about this," Tamara whispers to me.

"Sure about what?"

"About them turning my lyrics into a song."

I look at her like she's just grown moose antlers out of her eyebrows. "What?! What else are lyrics for?"

"Well, they're for songs and everything, of course. But this is a little dark. And personal."

We watch the boys improvising for a few seconds. Jacob starts to mumble the words in a cool melody.

"Don't you think the crowd will like covers better?" Tamara says.

"What crowd?"

"At the summer festival. They might relate to stuff they know better."

She's right. Most people, especially around here, love to hear songs they know. And we could play some well-known classic stuff—Beatles or the Stones. U2 is popular, obviously. We could get the crowd singing along, like they did on the bus. That would be cool. But...

"You look lost in thought," Tamara says. The boys are ignoring us, having transitioned into what I guess will be the chorus of this increasingly epic song.

"I think we should play originals. We should be making our own sound. If we play, say, a U2 song and the oldies in the crowd go wild, then they're going wild for U2, not us. What's the point of that?"

"But what if we play originals and they just sit there?" She's nodding her head in time to the music, a little smile growing on her face. "They sound really *good*," she says.

The boys play on, oblivious. Tamara and I abandon our argument as I plop down behind my drum kit and start with a simple pattern. She plugs in her mic and starts singing the chorus of her song as if she's sung it a million times. Miles and Jacob adjust their volumes, and soon we're blasting out "The Alien," a grungy ballad with blues overtones. Tamara sings her lyrics with a little Janis Joplin edge. Then, as though we've all tapped into some unspoken agreement, in the middle of the song we bust into power alt rock—like Nirvana meets Queens of the Stone Age but with more feedback. It rapidly turns into a rock bridge from the Devil's list of all-time greatest rock bridges. Jacob takes a wicked solo, and Tamara improvises some wild vocals, while Miles and I just look at each other, huge grins on our faces.

When Tamara dives into the last verse, we reach a new plane of musical existence. Everything disappears but us and our instruments. It's like the walls of the studio fall down and we're playing for all creation, at the beginning and end of the universe.

I look up from my drums to see Miles blissing out, his eyes closed, his fingers thrumming the bass strings. Tamara clutches the microphone like she's hanging on for her life and sings with such emotion that my heart aches. And Jacob—Jacob is staring at Tamara with his mouth hanging open, like a hungry dog. Now *that's* interesting. He catches me watching him and looks away quickly. Still, *very* interesting.

When the song is finished we're sweating, red-faced and laughing like maniacs.

"THAT WAS TOTALLY INSANE!!" Miles yells.

Even though Tamara is laughing too, she also looks like she wants to cry. Or hug someone. Possibly both. We're all in a weird post-uber-awesomeness daze.

I freaking LOVE this band.

Seven

"Check. Check." Miles tunes both guitars while Jacob checks the sound system. Tamara and I tighten all the bolts on my drum kit. I hate wobbly drums, so I like to have everything as tight as possible. I still can't quite believe Nate organized this for us. A lunchtime gig at his café? It's too awesome to be real. I'm too nervous to live. I need to do some yoga or something.

"Check. Test. One two. One two," Jacob says. He's one of those audio nuts who claims he can hear a difference between wool and polyester, so his soundchecks can sometimes be a bit tedious. "Check. Test. Chest. I mean, check. Check."

A curvy waitress sets Jacob's milkshake down on a nearby table while Tamara and I shake with laughter. Jacob laughs with us. "It was an honest mistake!" he says.

Nate comes by with a coffeepot and refills my cup. "Are you guys excited?"

I try to act cool, which is dumb, because trying to act cool almost always results in looking extremely *un*cool. Sometimes I think I should stop worrying about cool altogether.

"It's a small crowd," Tamara says, looking around Nate's workplace. Most of the tables have one or two people. Half of them seem to be working on laptops. The rest are watching us set up with bemused expressions on their faces.

"All right, I know," Nate says. "This whole lunchtime-gig idea may need to catch on a bit. You guys are trailblazers. This is totally going to be a thing."

Tamara doesn't look convinced. I'm not convinced either. Even at the table taken up by our four sets of parents, every eye is locked on a cell phone. Except for my mom. She's reading *Slaughterhouse-Five* again.

Just as Jacob finishes the soundcheck, my eyes are drawn to a table by the window. With the bright sunlight streaming in I can't quite make out who is sitting there but it looks like...

"Is that *Chad Banner*?" Jacob says, adjusting Tamara's microphone stand.

She glances over casually. "Oh, yeah. I Facebooked him. He was always pretty nice about how the whole Fants thing went down. Wanted to see how I was doing. I guess he'll find out."

I duck down behind my cymbals. Now I feel like we should sound like Paramore meets Green Day or Chad Banner will think I'm a liar. And we don't sound anything like Paramore meets Green Day. I grip my drumsticks with sweaty palms and take a last look at our set list. We open with some old-time rock 'n' roll, then bust out an early Police number that Tamara kills. Then a bit of Red Hot Chili Peppers, a Pearl Jam thing we do mostly acoustic, a couple of pretty trashy neo-punk covers and, finally, we're going to finish with Tamara's song, "The Alien." It's a chronological journey through awesome music.

I hope Chad Banner stays to the end.

When Tamara steps up to the mic she does that metamorphic thing again. She goes from slightly geeky, frumpily dressed ordinary girl to suave front woman of a wicked-cool band. It's like magic.

"Hi, everybody, welcome to the Coffee Pit. I'm Tamara and we are..." Her voice trails off.

Oh, shoot! We forgot to pick a band name! We were going to do it before we set up. How could I have forgotten that?

"...the band with no name," Tamara finishes a millisecond later. I've got to give it to her. That's a pretty good save.

She turns, cool as anything, and winks at me. I count the boys in and we start playing.

At first no one seems to notice us. But halfway through our second song, a couple of people have turned their chairs and closed their laptops. No one is exactly dancing on the tables, but no one is throwing anything either, so that's good.

After our third song, Tamara catches her breath while Miles and Jacob switch to acoustic guitars.

"How is everybody doing today?" she says. There's a low mumble in response. "I said, HOW IS EVERYBODY DOING TODAY?!" The crowd, such as it is, comes back with a loud cheer. Why does that work anyway? It's so dorky. Then Tamara introduces us one by one. Miles and Jacob get a few squeals from some tweeny girls drinking bright pink bubble tea in the corner. When my name comes up, there's polite applause. A fair bit of it seems to be coming from Nate.

I try not to grin. Because that would look stupid. And Mom would never let me hear the end of it. Oh well.

The acoustic number is a big hit. The punk numbers make Chad Banner smile. I can see his big cosmetically enhanced teeth from here. Predictably, Jacob breaks a string on the last punk number, so while he changes it, Tamara talks to the crowd again.

"Thank you all for coming out and being such a fun crowd. I want to thank the Coffee Pit for having us, and my brother, Nate, for organizing everything. Hi, Nate!"

He waves from behind the counter. I duck down behind my cymbals again, then try to cover that by pretending to check my bass-drum pedal.

Is it getting hot in here?

"For our last number we're going to do an original tune," Tamara says. "It's called 'The Alien' and we wrote it together as a band two weeks ago, so it means a lot to us. In other words—BE NICE!" The crowd laughs as Jacob plays the opening chords of the song.

The song has mellowed since that first time we played it. It's not quite as wild, and it's also more polished. But still very, very dark.

Halfway through the song I notice that Chad Banner is holding up his phone. Videoing us? That's awesome. I look over and see the tweeny girls doing the same. And so is Nate. And our parents. YouTube is going to be on fire with us tonight.

When we finish the song, the crowd goes wild. Well, as wild as a crowd of ten office workers, eight parents, three tweeny homeschoolers, three baristas and our town's biggest DJ can go. Which is to say not all that wild. But it's a nice feeling anyway. You can tell that they liked us.

As we're packing up, Chad Banner comes over and gives Tamara a friendly hug.

"That was great, kid. I mean that. What a cool sound." I peek over my drum kit, and he catches my eye. "Hey, Stella Wing. You don't sound anything like Paramore or Green Day. You're better."

He's teasing me, but I decide to go for it. "Do you think we'll get into the Parkland Festival?"

I expect him to encourage me, or use some pointless platitude like "Just do your best" or something, but instead he gets serious.

"I don't know. We've got a new sponsor this year, and they're super conservative. Your sound is awesome, but it might be too edgy for the festival. As much as I hate to say it."

I guess I'm not very good at hiding my disappointment. "There're bigger things than the festival though, kid," Chad says. "There's definitely a market for your sound. Just not the festival."

The boys have joined us, sitting on their amps, their guitar cases tucked between their knees. Like they're waiting for the Magical Mystery Tour bus to arrive.

"How old are you guys?" Chad says to them.

"Fourteen," the boys say in unison. Honestly, sometimes they're like Tweedledum and Tweedledee. It's embarrassing.

Chad looks thoughtful. "I see great things in your future," he says. "All of you. Let me know if you have any other gigs, okay? I'd like to come and check out your progress."

Then he leaves us, slipping on his sunglasses as he heads for the door.

* * *

Jacob's dad takes the boys and their gear in his sports car. Tamara and I get a ride with my mom because my dad has a meeting at city hall. The band is going to have a post-gig debriefing and maybe a little jam session before we plot our next move. So we head back to the studio.

"The show was great, girls," Mom says as we pull out of the parking lot.

"You think?" I say. "The crowd was pretty small."

In the backseat, Tamara has put her headphones on. She says she does that after performing to unwind a bit. Otherwise she's prone to "emotional outbursts." Possibly she means bursting into tears for no apparent reason. That sometimes happens to me.

"Twenty-five people is not such a small crowd," Mom says. "When Dad and I were first dating, we went to see this band called Deja Voodoo in this little joint in Richmond. For real, we were the only people there."

"God, that must have been awful for the band. How embarrassing."

"I don't know." Mom gets that nostalgic remembering-the-old-days look on her face. "We had fun. They had fun. We drank some beers together, they played some songs. It was okay."

"Why do you think nobody came?"

Mom pauses, stopping the car while some skateboarders roll across the road. "Deja Voodoo had a weird sound, for their time," she says. "And I guess in that part of the world people weren't into their music. But they had lots of fans elsewhere."

I think about that for a while. Tamara starts humming and half singing along to the soundtrack from *Hairspray* in that person-wearing-headphones way that's so funny. Mom and I smile at each other.

"Do you think Deja Hoodoo or whatever they were called should have played different music?" I ask Mom.

"What do you mean?"

"Well, if they'd played something a bit more mainstream, maybe they would have had more fans, and more people would have been there that night."

Mom pulls over in front of Dad's office. "But that was their sound. It was completely new, what they were doing. They were never huge stars, but they ended up being pretty influential. And they were true to their vision. Don't you think that's more important than being super popular?"

I nudge Tamara, who hasn't even noticed we've stopped. She jumps out of the car and heads around back to the studio, still humming and singing.

I think I'm starting to figure this out. "So it's like at school," I say to Mom. "To be popular and have tons of friends, you have to be kind of bland. But if you're yourself and a little, you know, edgy, you only have a few friends, but they're ones who really appreciate you?"

Mom gets a wet smile on her face and looks like she wants to cry. I can't think of anything more embarrassing than having to deal with a mom who is crying from pride, so I give her a quick kiss and mumble, "Thanks, Mom" before running away.

It's always so weird talking about important stuff with your parents.

When I get to the studio, Miles and Jacob are having a pretty big argument, for them. I mean, usually they love each other like they've been to war together, so this is serious.

"Because I want this to go somewhere," Jacob says. "Not everyone is going to medical school, you know."

"Just because my parents are doctors doesn't mean I want to be one," Miles says. "I'm just saying I don't want to sell out. We've only just started."

Tamara is watching quietly from behind my drum set. "What's going on?" I ask her.

"Jacob and I were talking about maybe writing some new stuff. Something a bit more poppy sounding. And Miles took offense at that because he's an *artiste*." She rolls her eyes.

"So you're saying sell out before we even have any credibility whatsoever?" Miles asks.

Tamara shrugs.

"*Do* you want to change our sound?" I ask her.

She shrugs again. "Look, I can sing anything. And I've been a pop star already, so I know what that's like. But I want to get into the festival, because I'd like to rub it into Fantalicious's collective smarmy face."

Jacob snorts a laugh, then covers his mouth.

"I don't think that's such great motivation for making musical choices," I say.

"Me neither," Miles says.

We fall silent. I'm starting to understand why awesome bands like the Beatles and the Police break up over "artistic differences." I never knew what that meant until this moment. I just wish we could have a few hit songs before it happens to us.

Eight

Sometimes I miss the days when I had normal, peaceful waking-up experiences. My mom or dad would come in and rub my back or stroke my hair, and when I rolled over they would say, *Time to get up, buttercup,* or something like that. They'd make breakfast for me, and it would all be like something out of an old picture book.

Now it seems like every morning is some new, bizarre world that I have to figure out. If it's not weird dreams or meowing phones, it's those mornings where you feel like maybe you've been drugged, because you're so groggy you can barely move. And then there's waking up with an urgent need to write a song. I mean so urgent that I have to write the lyrics down before I even pee. And I'm busting to pee so bad, I end up taking my notebook into the bathroom with me.

Once that's taken care of and four verses of lyrics and a chorus are written down, I pull out my guitar. I don't play guitar that well—enough to plunk out a few of the easier chords—but I can usually fake a little accompaniment, especially if the key is C. I take my guitar to the breakfast table and am taking bites of toast and figuring out my chords as Dad comes in, wearing his Sunday outfit. That is to say, his pajamas. We'll be lucky if he's dressed by four o'clock when my grand-parents come over for dinner.

"That's sounding good," Dad says as my song comes together. "What's it about?"

"I don't know. It came to me in a dream." I look down at my lyrics, analyzing them for the first time. "I think it's sort of a love song." Oh my god! Why did I say that? Now Dad's looking at me with a big, goofy smile on his face. If he says something about his baby girl growing up, I'm literally going to die. I shove toast into my mouth and escape out the back door before that can happen.

After strapping my guitar into the basket of my bike, I ride around aimlessly for a while, thinking about my song. And I keep thinking of Nate, which is infuriating. Finally, I can't stand it anymore, apparently, because I turn my bike in the direction of Tamara's house.

"Hey, Stell," Nate says as he opens the door. "Tammy's not here."

I stand there with about a million expletives running through my brain, none of which are helping me think of a way to get out of this with my dignity intact.

"Do you want to come in?" Nate says. "You look hot. I mean, sweaty, I mean, not in a bad way, just...do you want some juice or something?"

A few minutes later we're sitting on the front steps, sipping orange juice. "I just wrote a song. Do you want to hear it?" I ask him, more out of a desperate desire to break the awkward silence than because I actually want to play my song.

"I'd love to!"

Oh, Lord. Now I've done it. I pull my guitar out of my bike basket and strum the opening chords. But I only manage to sing one verse and half the chorus before my throat starts closing up like I've been stung by one of those killer bees.

"It goes on like that," I croak. "I haven't finished the rest of the verses." Lie. But necessary.

Nate smiles at me. "You have a pretty voice. It reminds me a little of Angie Hart."

"Wow. Thanks. That's an obscure comparison. But thanks."

"Tammy and I went through a *Buffy the Vampire Slayer* thing a few years ago." He shrugs and taps his forehead. "I have one of those memories that just keeps compiling things, like a giant database. You wouldn't believe the music trivia I've got up here."

"That's awesome. Hey, sometimes they have music-trivia night at the Youth Club. We should totally go next time."

What. The. Hell. Did I just ask Tamara's brother out on a date? No more juice for me.

Nate grins, two round pink patches growing on his cheeks. "That would be cool. I think we'd crush the competition, don't you?"

"Probably." If I was able to string a sentence together. Which I doubt.

Nate slurps the last of his juice and looks at a scampering squirrel on the lawn. "So did you come here to see Tammy or...?"

"Yes!" I yelp way too enthusiastically. "I mean, yes. I wanted to play her my song. Will she be back soon?"

"I'm not sure. She said she'd be at the church. Something about rehearsal. I have to go to work, but I can drop you there. You can put your bike in the back of the van."

Figures. He drives a minivan.

* * *

I wait for Nate to drive away before I open the church door. It would be just my luck for Tamara to come out right as he's leaving and see him. Then there would be all kinds of awkward questions about what I'm doing with her brother that would make me turn five thousand shades of red.

He does give me a little wave as he drives off though.

When I push the door open, I'm surprised not to hear the whole choir singing. I can only hear Tamara and an acoustic guitar. And it's not at all a church song. It's a schmaltzy old Shania Twain song that Mom used to make fun of. But Tamara's voice sounds sweet.

As I open the second door, from the vestibule into the church, I see a pair of sneakered feet poking out from behind the pews. They look familiar. Just then Tamara opens her eyes and sees me. She stops singing abruptly.

"Stella! What are you doing here?"

Beside her, emerging from behind the high pews, Jacob stands up.

I look at them both for a moment. Really, it's no big deal. Tamara wanted some singing practice and she asked Jacob to accompany her. It makes sense.

Except she wasn't singing any song that we do. Or any song that she would do in choir. And they both look guilty.

"What's going on?" I say.

"Nothing," Jacob says.

"We're just jamming," Tamara adds. Then there's an awkward silence. And awkward silences in churches are the worst because you feel like the whole holy family is judging you. I swear I see the statue of Mary roll her eyes.

"Okay, look," Jacob says. "We're just practicing a different sound. We figure if the punk band doesn't get into the festival, maybe a country-pop duo will."

I just stare at him, resisting the urge to punch him in the nose. "I don't understand," I finally say. "Are you guys quitting the band?" To my horror, I start to feel like I'm going to cry. I mean, Jacob is like a little brother to me, and Tamara—she's practically the best girlfriend I've ever had. And the band is my whole life!

"We're not quitting," Tamara says. "We're just covering the bases. Chad is right about our sound. It's too edgy for this gig."

"So you don't even want to try?"

"Of course we still want to try. This is just a backup plan."

Backup plans. The best way to suck the excitement out of almost anything. Backup plans are like diving off the high board with a parachute. I don't know why, but this bugs me. It's like I want it to be an "if we go down, we all go down together" kind of deal. Because how are we supposed to still be a band if Miles and I are shut out of the festival but Jacob and

Tamara are in? That won't be good for band morale.

I cross my arms. I know I'm doing the sulky face that Dad says will never win me any beauty contests, but I don't care.

"I don't see what the big deal is," Tamara says.

"No, you wouldn't."

"What's that supposed to mean?" Jacob says.

I glare at him because I think he should understand. "She's already been famous. She's already done tons of big gigs. She Facebooks Chad Banner like it's nothing. And she only wants to get into the festival for revenge. It's different for me."

Now it's Tamara's turn to cross her arms. "Yeah? How is it different?"

"I don't know. I guess I'm not a phony!"

You know when you look behind you and "too far" is already about a mile away? That's me. I expect Tamara to clock me one. Lord knows I deserve it. But instead, she speaks calmly and slowly as she packs her music sheets into a folder.

"You know, Stell, I wish *you* had been kicked out of Fantalicious. Then you'd know what phony is. Oh, except *you* wouldn't have been kicked out because, well, look at you."

Then she grabs her cardigan and her purse and stomps out. Jacob and I wait in silence as the heavy door swings closed behind her.

"You totally *would* have been kicked out of Fantalicious," Jacob says, snapping his guitar case closed. "You can't even sing."

I think of about a dozen nasty comebacks, but not until he's already followed Tamara out.

And I never even got to play them my song.

Nine

"Chad Banner's office, Mark speaking."
Click.
Really? Did I just hang up on Chad Banner's sexy-sounding assistant? What is the matter with me? I take a deep breath and dial again, counting backward from fifty million as I listen to the ringtones.

"Chad Banner's office, Mark speaking."

"Uh, hi, uh, is Chad...Mister Banner there?"

"Who may I say is calling?"

"Stella Wang—I mean Wing. Stella Wing."

"One moment, please."

The hold music is "Riders on the Storm." That's awesome. I get so into listening to it that I nearly fall over when someone finally picks up.

"Hey, Stella Wing," Chad Banner's easy voice says. "What's happening?"

"Nothing. I mean, not much. I mean...I had a few questions about the Parkland Festival auditions. Is it okay that I called?"

"Sure it's okay, kid. What do you want to know?"

Of course I don't know where to start or what exactly I want to know. So I just jump in feet first, no life jacket or anything.

"Do you think we should change our sound to get into the festival?"

"What?! No! Of course not. Your sound is awesome. It's really raw and real."

"But the festival selectors won't like it. Apart from you, I mean."

Then he curses, a bad one too, and apologizes profusely before clarifying. "Forget the festival selectors. It's just a dumb small-town corn festival anyway."

"Yeah, but it's the only gig in town. That *we're* likely to get. I mean, we won't be playing the ChepCo Arena anytime soon." The ChepCo Arena is a giant hockey rink that the local fertilizer depot sponsors. And fertilizer is about right for it too.

It smells bad, and most of the bands that play there are utter cr—

"That's the point, kid," Chad says, interrupting my chain of thought. "It doesn't need to happen anytime soon. You're still so young. Why not just wait awhile? Let things evolve."

I resist the urge to growl. I hate it when older people talk like this. Maybe I DO have my whole life ahead of me, but it doesn't feel like that. It feels like something amazing needs to happen NOW or I'm going to implode.

I change the subject. Slightly.

"What if we entered two acts? Like, one was the punk band, but then we did another act—say, an acoustic country-folk thing?"

Chad chuckles. "You'd think that would be sensible. Cover-the-spread kind of thing. But, unfortunately, every act in town seems to think that's sensible too. So we'd end up with one singer trying to audition eight times with eight different outfits. Finally, two years ago, the organizers changed the rules. One entry, one song, per performer. You can't even have a bass player in two different bands, which goes against everything natural in the universe if you ask me, but there it is."

Well. That sucks. I would explain why to Chad, but he interrupts me. "Listen, Stella, I'm on air in five minutes, so I have to go. But I'll see you at the tryouts, right?"

"I guess so," I say.

"You play as wild and edgy as you want, kid. Don't disappoint me." Then he hangs up.

So this is my life now. A month ago, if you had told me I'd one day be worried about disappointing Chad Banner, I would have said you were crazy.

* * *

Hours later I still haven't decided how to broach this subject with Tamara and Jacob. Text. Email. Phone call. Maybe I could try to find them. This town is not that big. It probably wouldn't take long. But they might not be together. Then the conversation would have to be had twice. Or I'd have to rely on one of them to fully inform the other of the festival regulations. That would give them all kinds of opportunity to talk behind my back about what a pain in the butt I am.

Yep. There's no doubt about it. I'm over-thinking this.

I go ahead and send a text to Tamara, Jacob and Miles.

Band meeting. Studio. Now.

It's a little megalomaniac, I know. And I fully expect at least one of them to text back that they're busy or possibly that I should shove my band meeting up my nose, but ten minutes later we are all at the studio, eyeing each other warily, like apprehensive cats.

"I spoke to Chad Banner today," I say, not bothering with a preamble.

"And?" Miles says.

Poor Miles. I forgot to update him on what's going on. I backpedal a bit. "Okay, so these two"—I point accusingly at Jacob and Tamara—"were preparing another set for the audition. Acoustic country folk or some crap."

Miles looks at Jacob as if he has just killed his favorite puppy. "What?"

"It was her idea," Jacob says.

I expect Tamara to get mad at him, but for some reason she just hoots with laughter.

"You big liar," she says with a snort. "You called me."

Jacob starts to babble defensively, and if I wasn't so mad at everyone, I would just sit back and enjoy it. "I only called you to...uh...I wanted to see...uh... if you wanted to practice...uh...something."

Honestly. I think his puberty hormones have addled his brain. Tamara gives him a sympathetic look. "Okay, fair enough. It was my idea to practice some new songs. But *you* suggested we audition with them."

"Only because you said you didn't think the band would get into the festival!"

Miles and I look at each other as if to ask "Do you think we should intervene?" I shrug. Miles puts his hands up. "Stop. Stop!" he yells. Tamara and Jacob fall silent. "We still haven't heard what Stella talked to Chad Banner about," he says.

I quickly explain about only being able to audition with one act. Tamara and Jacob exchange doubtful looks when I finish.

"Well, that's easy," Miles says. "We audition with the band. Real rock music for real people. That's our mission, right?"

"I told you it's not that simple," Jacob says. "We won't get in. We won't get to play. It will all be for nothing."

"But at least we'll make a point."

"A point for whom?" Tamara asks. "Three corporate judges who haven't got a clue, and Chad Banner, who's clearly already got the point."

"Maybe the judges will be won over," Miles says.

"Maybe I'll fly to the moon," Jacob says.

"Okay. OKAY! ENOUGH!" I can't stand it when people fight. I take a deep breath and try to exhale all the bad chi that's floating around the studio. "Let's take a vote, at least."

"It's going to be tied, Stella," Jacob says. "There are four of us."

"Yeah, I can count, Jake. Thanks. Let's *start* with a vote and see where we're at. Okay?" I take another breath. All I want to do is sit behind my drums and beat on them for a few hours, but this has got to be resolved. "All those in favor of going in hard and edgy. The band sound. The band songs." I raise my hand, and Miles quickly does too.

"Okay. Two votes for rock 'n' roll. All those in favor of a softer sound. Maybe some folky crap."

Jacob raises his hand tentatively. We all turn to Tamara. Her vote will either tie us or commit us once and for all to play the edgy sound at the audition. What she does next will affect everything.

She bursts into tears.

Jacob jumps up and puts his arm around her shoulder. "Hey. Hey, it's just a vote. It's no big deal. Really."

"I don't want it to be up to me!" Tamara says, sobbing.

I hate tears. Other people's even more than my own. But I think I must be growing up or something, because I'm getting less useless at human interaction every day. I duck behind my drum kit and grab the stool, moving it behind Tamara's butt. Jacob gently sits her down.

"I'm sorry!" she wails. Then she sobs some more.

Miles opens his backpack and digs out a chocolate bar. But when he holds it out to Tamara, she just cries even harder.

"That will just make it worse!"

"It's chocolate," Miles says insistently. "Chocolate makes everything better."

"Chocolate makes you fat!" Tamara shouts. Then she lets her head fall into her hands.

"I've gotten so fat. I'll never be a rock star or any kind of star!"

"You're not even a little bit fat," Jacob tries.

"What would you know?" Tamara lifts her head up so quickly that Jacob has to jump out of the way to avoid copping it in the chin. "You weigh about twelve pounds! And you eat everything."

Miles pulls a crumpled tissue from his pocket and holds it out, a little uncertainly, his earlier failure with the chocolate obviously still fresh in his mind. But Tamara takes it and blows her nose at an incredible volume. No wonder the girl can sing. She's got nasal cavities like canyons.

"It's because I started taking the birth control pill," Tamara says, sniffling.

Poor Miles and Jacob look horrified at this confession. Miles puts his hands over his ears and starts going "La la la la..."

"Not for that," Tamara says. "As if anyone would want me anyway. It was because my periods were so heavy and—"

"Girl talk!" Jacob says. "We're out of here." He grabs Miles, who is still singing to himself, and pulls him out the door. It slams behind them.

Tamara shakes her head ruefully. "Well, that was humiliating."

"It's fine. Boys don't understand that hormonal stuff. I mean, OUR hormonal stuff. They have their own problems, obviously—I mean, so I hear. No one is interested in me either."

Tamara snorts. "*Nate* is interested in you."

"*Jacob* is interested in you."

"No he's not. Is he? He's, like, four inches shorter than me."

"So, he'll grow. Probably. Do you like him too?"

"Do you like Nate?"

We look at each other and burst out laughing. It just seems so unlikely that we would suddenly be talking about boys like two normal girls. I mean, we're FAR from normal. Obviously.

"We still haven't decided what kind of music to play," I say as we settle down.

Tamara spins on my drum stool. "I know. To be honest, I prefer the harder stuff. It suits my mood right now." She shrugs, and I get the feeling that she's on the cusp of telling me what's really going on. "I just don't have the look that goes with the sound."

About fifty thousand protestations pour out of my brain, but, sadly, none of them make it to my mouth. So I just stand there, struck dumb. Finally, the ability to speak returns.

"Are you for real?" I say. It comes out a bit snippier than I mean it to. "I mean, that's what's making you unsure?"

"Why are you so surprised? We've talked about this before."

"I know, but..." The truth is, we *have* talked about it, but maybe I wasn't listening because I thought Tamara's thing was the same "I'm so fat" "No, I am" "No, I AM!" crap that the girls at school go on about incessantly. I just tune it out. I must have partially tuned out Tamara too, but this is obviously a big thing for her. So much that it's affecting her enjoyment of performing. "You're so *awesome* though, Tamara. I just don't know how you can be so under-confident."

Tamara sighs. "No? Well, skinny people never get it."

That stings a little, but I let her have it. She's probably right. It's always hard to imagine something you've never experienced. One day Miles and I might have to talk to Tamara about being black or Chinese in such a white town. But now's probably not the time.

"I don't care about the *look*," I say. "I just dress how I feel comfortable."

She looks like she doesn't believe me. Then she waves her hands down her pink cardigan and gray corduroy skirt. "This is how I feel comfortable. Can I perform dressed like this?"

"Why not? You did at the café the other day. You were epic."

"I'll look like an idiot. People will laugh at me."

"No one is going to be laughing after you start to sing."

Tamara smiles a bit then. If there's one thing she's confident about, it's the power of her voice. She reminds me of that dorky woman from England who sang on TV and got a hundred million YouTube hits. And while Tamara is thinking about what a kick-butt singer she is, I have to convince her that she can pull off the rocker-chick thing—but her way.

"Look," I say, pulling out my cell phone and doing a quick Internet search. "Here, look at k.d. lang. When she started making albums, female country singers all wore spangly dresses and push-up bras, and she had this crazy cowgirl look going on. Now she wears nothing but suits." I click on my phone a few times. "Or here—Annie Lennox. Performed at the Grammys dressed as ELVIS. With SIDEBURNS! And Björk. Look, she wore a goose to the Oscars!"

"I'm not wearing a goose."

We're shaking with laughter now.

"Look at Aretha! And Queen Latifah! They're terrific. And fat. You could fit two of you into Aretha's dress. But she's literally the queen of soul. And Janis Joplin! Check her out. When girl singers all had beehive hairdos and fake eyelashes, she didn't wear makeup or anything. She was so real she was unreal."

Tamara takes my phone and scrolls through a few pictures thoughtfully. "I'm sorry about before," she says finally. "I mean, about the crying and stuff. I'm just having one of those frail days."

"We all have frail days," I say, giving her an encouraging pat on the shoulder. "From time to time."

Ten

"Stella, I have two words for you," Miles says, piling clothes into my arms. "Zebra leggings."

"Oooh," I say, digging through the pile. I have a real weakness for animal prints. And leggings.

On the other side of the sale rack, Tamara sighs. She holds up a narrow leather skirt. "In what universe is this extra large?" Jacob patiently takes the skirt from her and hangs it back up. Then he gently steers her away.

We're in the Blue Mantle, the most awesome thrift store in a hundred miles. I had to beg my mom to drive us here because it's in a whole other town, but she finally agreed when I suggested she spend two hours at their weird little arts-and-crafts bazaar. Mom's weakness is crocheted dishcloths and pottery coffee cups. She can't get enough of them.

It was Miles's idea for us all to go shopping for audition clothes together. He even convinced his dad to sponsor us with fifty dollars each. All we have to do is put stickers for his laser-tattoo-removal service on all our cases. It's brilliant marketing, actually, when you think about all the tattooed wannabes who will be at the auditions. And fifty dollars goes a long way in the Blue Mantle because the women who volunteer here are about a hundred and fifty years old and don't know how much people normally pay for such rad clothes. The zebra leggings say *Made in the United Kingdom*, for God's sake! And they're five bucks! I have to have them.

Miles comes out of the fitting room in a pair of brown cords and a paisley shirt. He manages to look like a young Lenny Kravitz and the ghost of Jimi Hendrix at the same time.

"I'm totally performing barefoot," he says, admiring his reflection in the large gilded mirror.

"Live your dreams, kid," I tell him. I've decided on the zebra leggings, a men's black shirt that goes down to my knees, and a child's double-breasted waistcoat that I can barely do up. It's lime green and has bumblebees on the buttons! I'm going to wear my biker boots with the outfit, I think. Docs would be too predictable.

After we pay, Miles and I search for Jacob and Tamara. We find Jacob standing outside the fitting rooms in the back of the store. He's wearing a surprisingly well-fitting men's suit and looking pretty much like one of the Beatles. Which is excellent in every possible way.

"Where's Tamara?" I ask. Jacob points toward a closed fitting-room door. I have a flashback to the day I tried to shop with her, when nothing fit and everything made her look sad. I hope we're not facing a repeat.

"When are you coming out?" Jacob says to the door.

"I'm not sure about the dress," Tamara says. "I kind of had to squeeze into it."

Jacob grins. "The best dresses always have to be squeezed into."

"Jacob!"

He looks at me innocently. "What? It's true!"

"Okay, I'm coming out," Tamara says.

I actually hold my breath as the door opens.

Ever have one of those moments when you suddenly see the universe as a friendly, supportive haven instead of a hostile and confusing maze of dark tunnels and dead ends? Seeing Tamara in that dress is like that. She looks A-MA-ZING! She is definitely squeezed into the dress up top, and her boobs are framed in wild waves of ruffles. The skirt is gathered and full and cloudy-looking, like cotton candy. She's wearing it over black tights, with green Chucks on her feet. The dark pink of the dress, her pale skin and fair hair, which she's bunched into a pair of spiky pigtails, all work together to create an arty, rocky, sexy hipster look that I could never in a million years pull off.

I turn to look at the boys, to see their reactions. Miles is grinning and clapping. Jacob's face is bright red, his mouth hanging open. I'm calling that a win.

"How do you feel?" I ask Tamara as she considers her reflection.

She takes her time answering, even swirls in the dress, before offering her assessment.

"I feel like a star," she says. "An exploding pink star."

"You mean in a good way, right?"

Tamara doesn't answer. She just ducks back into the fitting room and grabs her purse.

Five minutes later, when we all leave the store, Tamara is still wearing the dress.

* * *

When we get back to town, Mom drops us at Mitchell Music, our only store that sells musical instruments. The staff used to be mad-conservative, classical-only jerks who sneered at kids like us if we didn't buy something straight away. But recently the store got a new manager, a cool Jamaican guy with dreadlocks and a wicked accent. He's a lot more tolerant. And, perhaps not coincidentally, there are now a lot more girls in the store whenever I drop in.

I need some drumsticks, and the boys need strings. Tamara comes along to peruse the sheet music. I guess we've been having such a magical shopping day, we don't want it to end.

Mitchell Music has a great selection of used guitars, which the boys dive into without so much as a see-you-later. I'd love to try the drum set on display, but that might be a bit antisocial. Instead, Tamara and I head into the sheet-music part of the store.

"I want to learn an aria," she says, flipping through the classical-vocals section. "Actually, I might do a tenor aria. 'Nessun Dorma,' maybe."

Always with the contradictions, this girl. I love it.

"Tammy? Oh my god!" a sickly sweet voice says behind us. I turn around just as four girls dive onto Tamara and smother her in air kisses and squealy girl hugs. Once they step back, I recognize them. They're the remaining members of Fantalicious, all four of them in booty shorts, tight cartoon T-shirts and way too much makeup. They look like they should time-travel back to the nineties and dance in a Britney Spears video.

Tamara introduces me, and the Fants are a little too friendly as they look me up and down.

"OMG, I totally used to do karate with you, Stella," says one of them. "You don't recognize me?"

"Did you kick me really hard in the head the last time you saw me? Maybe that's why I can't place you," I say, which makes them all squeal with laughter.

Tamara catches my eye, her eyebrow raised. "What are you guys doing here?" she asks.

Karate Girl answers. "We're looking for a song to cover for the Parkland Summer Music Festival auditions."

Another girl finishes her thought. "We think a cover will be a more popular choice. Apparently the judges are super conservative this year. Petra said even the Dixie Chicks would be too radical! Can you imagine?"

"What are *you* doing here, Tammy?" a third girl asks.

I begin to feel like we're having a conversation with some hideous four-headed beast.

Tamara hesitates. "I'm just looking at arias. I thought I'd try to learn one."

"Opera?" Karate Girl says. "Well, you know what they say about opera."

It's like watching a child fall down and knock her teeth out. Like you reach out to try to stop it, but you can't, even though it seems to be happening in slow motion. On cue, one of the other girls snorts.

"Yeah, it's not over until the *fat* lady sings."

Wow. Tamara is many things that these girls aren't, not the least of which is *dignified*. She just turns and looks down at the selection of arias as though the last five minutes didn't even happen. Maybe she's thinking how she would mop the floor with all of them in a real singing competition if it ever came to that. Maybe she's just trying to keep from crying or punching one of them in her frosty-pink mouth.

As for me, I don't care about dignity. "You know what they say about trashy pop music?" I ask the four girls, noting with some satisfaction that they all look vaguely mortified. "It's not over until the *cheap skank* sings."

Then I grab Tamara's hand and drag her back toward the guitar section.

"Thanks," she says, giving my hand a squeeze.

"Believe me, it was my pleasure. Are you okay?"

"I'm fabulous," she says. "I'm a pink exploding star, and the singer in the best band since Sonic Youth."

The boys are having a little jam session when we get there. I look at the manager with a pleading expression, and he just rolls his eyes and shrugs. The display drum set is pretty sweet. It has Zildjian cymbals and a wicked run of toms that I'm itching to try out. I dig my drumsticks out of my backpack and start a simple rhythm to go with Miles and Jacob's jam. When Tamara plugs a microphone into the little PA, the boys automatically bust into her song, "The Alien." But she doesn't sing along.

"Wait!" she says into the microphone. Everyone in the store, including the Fants, who are still skulking around in the sheet music, turns to look at us. "Let's do the new one. Stella's song."

Oh, crap. My "love" song. We've only practiced it a few times since Nate blabbed about it to Tamara. To be honest, her voice makes it all kinds of sweet. Like sweet-love-song sweet AND sweet-edgy-moody-dark-and-broody sweet. That's the miracle of Tamara Donnelly.

I take a deep breath and count us in. "One, two, one two three four."

The song is basically an answer to Tamara's "The Alien." Where she wrote about feeling isolated and unworthy of someone who might love her, I wrote about how it feels when you finally meet that one person who seems to get you just as you are. The day I wrote it, I thought maybe it might be about Nate, which is mortifying beyond all measures of mortification. But as Tamara sings the opening lines, I begin to think that maybe I was writing about her. I mean, not in a romance way or anything, because I'm pretty sure I prefer boys. And I'm pretty sure Tamara does too. But she does get me better than almost anyone I've ever met.

A small crowd starts to gather around us as the song builds. Tamara comes around the back of the drums and stands beside me as she starts the chorus. She leans down to share the microphone with me. Without even thinking about it, I add a harmony to the chorus. Not only are the notes I randomly add amazing—all minor and introspective-sounding—but my voice comes from somewhere deep inside me that I didn't even know existed. I don't sound like a scared little girl. I sound like a *woman*. Miles and Jacob actually turn around, looking at us with their eyes bugging out.

I'll never be a singer like Tamara. I don't even want to be. But singing harmony with her in front of all these people, without squeaking like a mouse, running out of steam or just generally freaking out? It's for real just about the coolest thing that has ever happened to me. I don't even care about the music festival right now.

Watching the Fantasy Lickers sneak out with their skinny tails between their legs doesn't hurt either.

Eleven

t's audition day, and I'm not nervous, not one little bit.

Yeah. Right. I'm not a liar pants on fire either.

There's a band playing that is doing the very Shania Twain song I caught Jacob and Tamara practicing three weeks ago. And they're good too. The guitarist takes a solo in the bridge that makes Jacob bite down on the guitar pick in his mouth.

"That's all skill and no spirit," Tamara says, patting his knee. "Anyone can copy a solo. Your solos are pure creative genius." She lets her hand linger on his knee for a few extra seconds. Jacob blushes to the tips of his ears. Miles, oblivious, tunes his bass with his headphones on.

We're tucked into a corner in the hallway outside the audition room. The festival organizers booked a large reception room in one of the business hotels. We all turned up at dawn and got a number. Now each act is waiting its turn out in the halls. Some in groups. Some by themselves. Some being fussed over by wild-eyed stage moms. It's just like *American Idol* but with fewer cameras.

So far I've been surprised by the quality of the acts auditioning. None of them are playing the kind of music I like, but there are some talented musicians around here. I guess I never opened my eyes and ears to that before.

The Shania Twain act finishes its song, and silence once again descends on the hallway. One of the organizers pokes his head out the door.

"Fantalicious?" he says. "FANTALICIOUS?"

Four girls in tight dresses appear around the corner, teetering on their high heels as they rush to the door.

"You're on deck. Wait here and come in when this next song ends."

Great. Now they're standing five feet away from us while the act before them plays.

The opening chords to "Viva la Vida" pulse through the thick wooden door.

"God help us," Tamara says. "I am so sick of this song."

"What song are you guys doing?" one of the Fants asks. It might be the girl I did karate with. They have all sort of blended into one, so it's hard to tell. They're wearing silver dresses with fishnet tights and high-heeled red Mary Janes over turquoise knee-high socks. I'm not sure if they are hoping to blind the judges or planning for an alien invasion.

"We're doing an original," Tamara answers lightly, as though these girls are decent human beings deserving of respect and not stuck-up brats. "I wrote the lyrics and the band wrote the music."

The Fants exchange a look. "We're doing a Kelly Clarkson song," one of them says, even though no one asked. "One of the judges went to her concert in Winnipeg last month. She tweeted about it. Petra researched them all."

I am so tempted at that moment to lie, to tell them that Tamara and I both had affairs with Chad Banner or something equally implausible, that

I actually feel it like a blob of gum stuck in my throat. As usual, Tamara rescues me from myself.

"That's clever. Well, good luck with it," she says.

I get the feeling the Fants are a little disappointed by Tamara's reaction. They stand around looking ridiculous for the rest of the song, which, mercifully, ends after only three verses. Someone holds the door open and they disappear inside.

"Kelly Clarkson?" I say. "Ew."

"I like her," Tamara says with a smile. "At any rate, I'm glad they picked her. She's got a killer voice, and none of those girls can live up to her standards. So I can sit here and feel smug while they suck."

Jeez. Tamara has a nasty side. I like it.

We stop talking. The boys stop tuning. I don't know why, but I think we're all waiting to hear what Fantalicious will sound like. It's weird, too, because it's not like they're our competition or anything. I mean, it's totally possible that we'll both get chosen for the festival, right?

Then I get nervous again, because what if Fantalicious is actually good? Maybe they grew souls or something and can actually perform decent music. I'm sitting here wanting them to suck because that might be the final cherry on the cake I've been building to feed Tamara's self-esteem. She wants to hear them fail. I want to hear them fail. But I'm not sure hearing someone else fail is a good way of feeding self-esteem. Just like cakes with cherries on top of them taste good but aren't all that good for you.

The music starts inside the audition room. It's "Already Gone," a super-schmaltzy song, but one that definitely needs a good singer. Tamara turns her ear toward the door as one of the Fants starts singing.

"Remember all the things we wanted..."

Crap. She sounds pretty good.

I watch Tamara's face. She has a little frown of concentration. Not upset or anything, but she definitely notices the singer's voice.

"Hmm, someone's been taking lessons," she says. "I wonder who her teacher is."

"You're better than her," I say automatically. It's true and everything, but I say it without even thinking.

Tamara tilts her head at me with a little smile. "Yeah, I know," she says. "But who cares? This is all a popularity contest anyway."

That takes a second to process. "What, you mean *this* contest is? Like, this audition?"

"This *business*, Stella. At the end of the day, talent only gets you so far. Sometimes you don't even need talent. Plenty of crappy millionaire performers out there."

I stare at her in her pink dress and pigtails, sitting cross-legged like some kind of froufrou mountain sage. Miles and Jacob have wandered down the corridor and are now fighting with the snack machine.

"So what's the point, then?" I ask Tamara. "What are we doing this all for, trying to be so good and so genuine, if none of it matters?"

Tamara looks at me for a few seconds and I realize that Fantalicious has finished their song. I hear them giggling before they all spill back into the hallway, clinging to each other and ignoring us as they wobble off. Their shiny silver butts disappear around the corner just as the next act begins its song inside the audition room. "Viva la Vida." *Again.*

"The *music* matters, Stella," Tamara says firmly. "You're the one who made me think about the music again. I got so twisted about the Fants and screaming tweens that I forgot it's the music that matters. Don't we just do this because it feels good?"

"I guess. Yeah."

"Well then. Take it from me, screaming tweens get real tiring after a while."

A head pops out of the audition room. I blink at it a few times before I realize it's Chad Banner.

"Stella Wing," he says. "I'm so glad to see you here."

"Aren't you supposed to be judging?" Tamara says, giving him a little shove with her sneakered foot.

"Nah, I can't stand Coldplay. I've recused myself."

Tamara and I both stifle laughs.

"Listen," Chad goes on. "You guys are on deck. Come on in and wait at the back, okay?"

Tamara jumps up and jogs down to the snack machine to muster the boys.

"Nervous?" Chad says as we wait for them to come back.

"Not really," I say and am surprised to realize it's not a lie. "I mean, I don't think the selectors will like our style, so we're just going to..." Not sure what. Maybe something that can't be articulated.

"Have fun?" Chad offers.

"Bigger than that," I say. "Be real."

Chad grins so widely that his bright white teeth nearly blind me. "Right on," he says, holding the door for us as Tamara and the boys run back from the end of the hall. I follow them into the audition room and Chad steps in behind me, letting the door swing closed. He ushers us to some chairs by the door.

"Give 'em hell, kid," he whispers before turning to head back to the selectors' table. Then he stops. "Oh, I nearly forgot. You didn't fill in a band name on your entry form. You want me to add it?"

"Sure," I say, giving Tamara a wink. "We're called the Frail Days."

Twelve

Waiting to hear the results of our audition is like torture dreamed up just for
me. As the weeks roll by, we try to keep
rehearsing in the studio as though nothing big
is hanging over our heads, but it's hopeless. We
keep stopping in the middle of songs because one
of us thinks we hear a phone ring. And we used
to have a strict phones-off rule for rehearsals, but
that's out the window, I guess.

Tamara and I have been hanging out almost
every day, writing songs and talking about music.
This morning, it's so hot in my room that we dare
each other to put on swimsuits and go to the
pool. I change into board shorts with skulls on
them and a sports bra thing. Tamara stops by her
house to put on a frilly little skirt suit that makes

her look like Betty Boop. The pool is packed with tanned teenage boys who keep looking over at us and nudging each other. What's that about anyway? Okay, so maybe we look ridiculous and my knees are getting sunburned, but it's fun.

As we're walking home, we talk about the summer festival for the millionth time.

"Two weeks isn't much time to prepare," Tamara says.

"No, I know. But I guess that means we'll hear today or tomorrow."

We don't say anything for about three blocks, both of us just trying to keep from exploding, I guess. We're standing in front of my house when Tamara speaks again.

"I'm freaking out. Are you?"

"Not at all," I lie, nodding my head stupidly. Tamara laughs. I'm about to ask her if she wants to make lemonade when my phone rings. I dig it out of my backpack while Tamara clutches at me.

Chad Banner says the caller ID. I turn the phone around to show Tamara. She practically draws blood, digging her fingers into my shoulder.

I'm close enough to my home wireless that the call actually comes through as a video call.

I press *accept* and Chad's grinning face comes into view. He's obviously sitting at his desk, calling from his laptop.

"Hey, ladies! It's both of you!"

"Hi, Chad!" we say. Actually, it comes out more like a joint squeal.

"Listen, I have good news and bad news."

Gahh! Why is it *always* that way? Why can't it ever be good news and more good news?

"Okay, shoot," Tamara says, releasing her claw hold on my shoulder. "Start with the bad news."

Chad takes a breath. Behind him I can see a few details of his sleek office. It must be in that new high-rise downtown. If you can call ten stories a high-rise.

"Here's the thing. You didn't get selected for the festival."

I want to yell "WHAT?!" indignantly, but I'm not surprised. I glance over at Tamara. Her lips are pressed together. She knew this was a likely outcome too, but it's still disappointing.

"So what's the good news?" I say.

"I don't want to get your hopes up before I check one thing. How old are you guys again?"

"The boys both just turned fifteen. Tamara is sixteen now and so am I."

Chad looks thoughtful. "Let me go make another call. Here, talk to Mark."

Chad gets up and steps offscreen as an extremely handsome young man sits down in his place.

"Thanks for holding for Chad Banner, the king of coolville," he says smoothly. "Your call is important to us. Please hold the line." Then he starts singing "The Girl From Ipanema" as cheesy hold music, making silly faces.

Tamara and I burst out laughing, which helps dissolve some of the disappointment of Chad's bad news. Mark just keeps singing, oblivious. Chad comes back into view, his cell phone to his ear.

"You're sure?" he says. "Well, yeah, we can work around that. Thanks." He pockets the phone and puts his hand over Mark's mouth. "You're ridiculous," he says, shoving him away before turning to us. "So, here's what I've cooked up for you..."

Then he starts talking super fast about a record label and liquor licenses and getting the carry-over from a big festival up north and some executive who saw us on YouTube and doing a guest spot on his radio show and he wants to be our manager. He's talking so fast I can barely grasp everything he's saying. Also, my shoulder hurts. I look down to see that Tamara has grabbed me again and is pinching so hard her knuckles are bright white.

Wait. Chad Freakin' Banner wants to be our *manager*?

"Well?" Chad asks with a bright grin. "How does that sound?"

Two seconds later my parents run out of the house to see what all the screaming is about.

* * *

There's a moment when I'm drumming when the problems of the world seem to evaporate. Then the world evaporates, and it's just me and the music. And that's the moment when I forget all the stuff about getting famous or making money. Because I feel like I could live forever in those beats, in that rhythm. That's when I feel most like a musician and not just some lame, idealistic kid.

It happens when I play by myself in my room, and it happens when I jam in the studio with the band. It even happened when we auditioned for the summer festival. I think we all lost ourselves in the music so much that none of us cared about the blank looks on the judges' faces when we finished. Chad was grinning his bright white smile again. The other three judges looked a bit fright- ened. But we didn't care. We'd found that place despite everything. That magical musical place. To hell with them if they couldn't go there with us.

I'm in that place right now. I thought the crowd would distract me—the people dancing, the glasses clinking, the lights, the faint smell of cigarette smoke drifting in from the terrace. But none of it seeps into our secret world. We're in our moment, in the zone where it's clear that music fixes everything.

Tamara is singing "The Alien," belting it out like her life will end if she doesn't break every window in the building. And Jacob is tripping out on a riff he pulled in his solo that made my eyes fill with tears. And Miles, in his bare feet and paisley shirt, is hopping and popping bass notes like they're celestial thunderbolts.

That's right. The *zone*. The Frail Days are on fire.

Who cares if we didn't make the Parkland Summer Music Festival? I mean, *who cares*? This is a million times more awesome. We're playing in Chad Banner's nightclub. A nightclub! We're not even allowed off the stage because we're all underage. We have to climb out onto the roof and get back to the dressing room that way so we don't have to cross through the licensed area. That's so punk rock.

I open my eyes and see Chad Freakin' Banner drop a bottle of champagne on the table of some guys in flashy clothes. Tamara says they are execs from a big music label. She met them when she was in Fantalicious. Just looking at them now, drinking champagne and schmoozing with Chad—our *manager*, Chad—makes me see stars. Not stars like they're going to make me a star, but stars like I'm going to faint face first into my snare drum. I close my eyes and crank my drumsticks down for the last verse of "The Alien."

Once my parents told me on Christmas morning that we were going to Disneyland. We took a limo to the airport, with the Beatles blaring the whole way. I wore my pirate costume on the plane. It was sunset by the time we arrived at Disneyland, and then there were fireworks and a huge parade. Darth Vader was in the parade. That was a pretty good day.

But this blows Disneyland far out into the Pacific Ocean. What. A. Rush. And looking down to the table where all our parents are sitting, I can tell they must be feeling the same way. They're practically neon with pride.

We reach the last bar of the song, Tamara holding on to the final note like it's a life preserver. Then I slam my sticks down on the cymbals, busting us all out of magical music land with a resounding crash. There's a beat that feels like being punched in the chest, and then the whole club explodes into applause.

Holy crap. Wicked.

Soon they're stamping their feet and banging beer bottles on tables. Tamara pulls me to the front of the stage with the boys, and we all take repeated bows to the tune of a club full of half-drunk goths, punks and rockers. Where Chad finds all these people I'll probably never know.

A camera flash pops. Then another one. Blinking the spots from my eyes, I see that one of the cameras belongs to an executive from the champagne table. I have to have a little talk with myself, trying to come down from the "omigod we're going to be famous" cloud that's threatening to carry me away. Despite everything—the cheering and the flashing cameras and the smell of beer—I need to keep it real.

It's pretty hard at moments like this.

As the crowd begins to settle, Chad jumps up onto the stage, taking the microphone.

"Let's hear it for the FRAIL DAYS!" he yells. The crowd erupts again. As Chad high-fives us all, I notice that Tamara and Jacob are holding hands. And Jacob seems to have grown about four inches since the last time I took a good look at him. Before I can process this there's a flurry of bright color as Nate climbs out onto the stage (from the roof—he's underage too!) with an armful of flowers. He hands a giant bouquet to Tamara. The crowd goes "aw" as he gives her a brotherly hug and kiss on the cheek. Then he turns to me, a single rose left in his hand.

Uh...this is...kinda cool too. I'm pretty sure my face must be glowing red though. If I was another girl, I might be thinking that dreams really *do* come true.

Okay, maybe that's a little more princess than punk, but just this once I think I'll let it slide.

Acknowledgments

It is not easy being a young performer. Combine the insecurity of youth with the uncertainty of the creative artist and put it on display in front of hundreds of people, and you get a whole lot of craziness. Yet we artists stick with it, despite the humiliating auditions, the empty seats, the rejection letters, the bad reviews. We stick with it because we are called to it, because we believe that *this* is what we have to give back to the world.

You would think that young performers, exceptional as they often are, would get all kinds of support from the adults around them, but such is often not the case. "Have something to fall back on" is the frequent mantra. "You'll never make any money at it." For kids who have heard these discouraging words repeatedly, hearing a little of the opposite can be like elixir to the creative soul. So I'd like to acknowledge the few adults who encouraged me when I was a young artist. I won't name you; you know who you are. Thank you.

And to all you young artists out there—you're terrific.

GABRIELLE PRENDERGAST is a UK-born Canadian/ Australian who lives in Vancouver, British Columbia, with her husband and daughter. She holds an MFA in Creative Writing from the University of British Columbia. A part-time teacher and mentor, Gabrielle is the author of the verse novels *Capricious* and *Audacious*, which was shortlisted for a CLA Award. Gabrielle blogs and rants at www.angelhorn.com and www.versenovels.com.

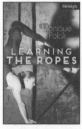

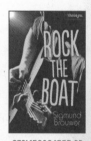